Presenting Princess Solei on Her First Birthday

The Magic in Her Smile

Shangri-La Durham-Thompson

ISBN: 978-1-957956-28-2 (sc)
ISBN: 978-1-957956-29-9 (e)

Rev. date: 08/19/2022

Presenting

Princess Solei on Her First Birthday

Shangri-La Durham-Thompson

Dedication

For my granddaughter, Nina Solei whose smile lights up our lives. May your smile continue to bless others and may God bless your life. And to:

My parents, Julia Durham, JP and Coolidge Durham (deceased), who raised us to be all that God wants us to be.

Nina's other grandmother, my friend, Debra Francis who cares for her everyday.

My siblings, Rev. Coolidge 'Danny' Durham (and his wife Paula), Dr. Donna Durham-Pierre (and her daughter, my niece, Kenya) and Mrs. Shelby Durham-Jackson, CEO of At Home Health ... my rocks.

My exceptional husband, Stanton Thompson Sr. who pushed me in this endeavor.

My wonderful sons Stanton Jr. and Shan-on (and Shan-on's wife, Dr. Nyshawana Francis-Thompson, Nina's parents).

My nephew Coolie, Nina's special godfather.

Nina's special cousins: Nyla, Shyla, BJ, Zorian, Norico and others too numerous to mention.

My extended family (aunts, uncles, cousins, and friends).

Please know that I love and value you all.

Keep smiling.

Shangri-La

She came into our lives, you see,
one chilly winter's morn,

And the world changed for the better
because Nina Solei was born.

Yes, babies are so precious,

And just like you, my child,

They are such family blessings

And small for just a while.

It seemed like only yesterday that
this loving child was born.

But it had been a whole year
since that February morn.

February, the month of love,

She was our Valentine.

Her birth has brought us so much joy.

She impacts hearts and minds.

To celebrate her one year's birth,

Like we will do for you,

Her mother told those far and near,

As parents often do.

Her birthday invitations

Were sent to all, it seemed.

Posted on the social network–

I never could have dreamed.

Her birthday cake,

Delectable,

Was the best they could afford,

And the venue they selected,

Was one that she adored.

Balloons

were

floating

everywhere

Like clouds up in the sky.

The atmosphere, so magical,

It almost made me cry.

Oh, I wish you could have seen her

In her gown of shimmering blue,

Her hair just like a halo

Under a crown that sparkled too.

And when she made her entrance

In her pink Cadillac,

Those assembled oohed and aahed.

And when she smiled, we all smiled back.

The music they selected for
her entrance in the hall

Acknowledged she was dazzling
as did her photos on the wall.

The whispers, "she's a real princess"

Were heard throughout the room.

Her smile was huge, her eyes were bright,
and her cheeks like a full moon.

Sweetie, just like her, I hope that
you will always smile at me.

Smiles melt the heart and make
our world a better place to be.

Yes, Solei was a special gift sent
from heaven up above.

Her presence on this place called
earth just proves to us God's love.

I'll hug you now.

Oh, hug me back,

As tightly as you can,

And give to me your special smile,

For smiles attract a friend.

Nina greeted all her guests
with her exquisite smile.

And then she hugged a little boy
she'd not seen in a while.

I wish you'd seen her poppie's face

As he held her in his arms.

It shone just like a lighthouse.

Yes, he beamed, he too was charmed.

Her poppie named her princess

Because when she first smiled at him

He said he felt electrified

And his heart had jumped within.

Grandma D, her babysitter beamed
Throughout the whole event.

26

When her smile lessened pain in

Great Grandma Durham,

We confirmed,

She was heaven-sent.

HAPPY
BIRTHDAY
APP
Nina Solei
ONE

Her aunts, uncles, cousins, and
friends were at the party too.

They all took pictures of her,
like we will do for you.

Princess Solei
Princess Solei
Princess Solei
Princess Solei
Princess Solei
ICE CREAM
Vanilla

There was pizza, cake and ice cream,
party hats, and bags for all,

And the children who attended
just had themselves a ball.

They painted colored pictures
and rode the carousel,

And they just had a grand ol' time.

This wasn't hard to tell.

The decorations were fabulous,

But far above all this

Was the fact that this darling princess
Had brought the world such bliss.

One can't deny the magic in
the twinkle of her eye

Or dismiss the way she makes us feel
Or explain the reason why.

There's acceptance and there's healing
in the smile that Solei gives

Her smile lowers stress in everyone
and teaches us to live.

Although we gave her presents,
they could not compare

To the gift that her smile gave to us,
although she was unaware.

I think babies are sent from heaven

To bring happiness to earth.

I believe they're proof of our God's love,

So we should welcome each child's birth.

Now, smile at me, my little one.

You can be a prince or a princess too

If you smile that smile that
melts our hearts.

Making us smile back at you.

And when your birthday comes this year

We will certainly celebrate.

And we'll smile for a smile's contagious,

A behavior to emulate.

When I think of Solei's birthday

And the gift that this princess brought,

It demonstrated that a simple smile

Has real value that should be taught.

So smile at me, my precious one,

Just smile and smile.

Just smile.

About the Author

Dr. Shangri-La Durham-Thompson, an avid reader, first began reciting poetry as a young child. In elementary school, she recalls reciting poems such as Paul Revere's Ride and Hiawatha, by Henry Wadsworth Longfellow. In high school, she recited the works of Paul Laurence Dunbar and Langston Hughes. Her love for the spoken word led her to study Speech and Drama Education and upon graduation, she taught in an elementary school for two years. She later taught English, Communication and Drama at the high school level for sixteen years, after obtaining her Master's degrees. After twenty years of teaching in the public school system, she became an Arts Education Officer for the Department of Education. She has served as acting middle school principal and was an elementary school principal for twelve years. She has taught Public Speaking and Communication at the Bermuda College and today she serves as an Education Officer for the Arts and Leadership at the Bermuda Department of Education. Shangri-La believes her name is prophetic as Shangri-La means eternal youth and beauty. In her younger years, she painted and sold visual art work. She has written and produced numerous plays and is the host of a weekly radio leadership program, *The Need to Lead.* Dr. Durham-Thompson served in her local church school as a teacher and superintendent for over thirty-years. She is married to Stanton Thompson Sr. They have two sons, Stanton Jr. and Shan-on. Nina Solei makes her a proud grandparent.